WRITTEN and ILLUSTRATED BY SANDY SPROTT

LITTLE KICKER

VISITS DOCTOR QUICKWELL

God answered my prayer.

This
LiTTLe KiCKeR booK
is Presented to

_____

NAME

by

_____

NAME OF RELATIVE, FRIEND, CHURCH OR ORGANIZATION

_____

OCCASION   DATE

Little Kicker Visits Doctor Quickwell

Published by Kimble Creek Press LLC, Hermitage, Missouri
Cover and text design by Amy Cole, JPL Design Solutions
Editing by Sam Sprott & Don Ginnings

Publisher's Cataloging-in-Publication data
Sprott, Sandy.
Little Kicker Visits Doctor Quickwell / Sandy Sprott.
p. cm.
ISBN 978-0-9843956-4-4 (Hardcover)
ISBN 978-0-9843956-5-1 (pbk.)
Summary : Little Kicker was afraid to get his donkey shots. The Lord sent Becky the Bunny to make him laugh
and chase away his fears.
[1. Donkeys --Fiction. 2. Physicians --Fiction. 3. Medical care --Fiction. 4. Christian fiction.] I. Title.
PZ7.S7688 Li 2013
[E] --dc23   2013907036

Manufactured by Color House Graphics, Inc., Grand Rapids, MI, USA
First Printing .... May 2013
Second Printing .... August 2018

MADE IN
U.S.A.

www.LittleKicker.com

This book is dedicated to our granddaughter, Rachael. You were born with red hair, and in this series of books about Little Kicker you are Rachael the Little Red Hen. I painted you with a lot of hearts because of all the love you give your family. Papa Sam and I love you beyond the rim of time.

"Look," said Mother Donkey,
"Farmer John is waiting for us."

"Yes," Hee Hawed Little Kicker,
"but I am hungry!"

6

"Meee Tooo," whinnied
Tony the Pony.

Mother Donkey answered,
"After you get your shots,
you can eat some delicious
new clover."

Little Kicker asked,
"What are shots?"

Mother Donkey replied, "Doctor Quickwell gives shots to help us from getting sick."

Tony the Pony added, "I know about shots. Doctor Quickwell takes a needle that is attached to a tube with medicine.

Doctor Quickwell sticks the needle through our hide. The medicine goes from the tube through the needle into our bodies."

9

Little Kicker, Tony the Pony and Mother Donkey walked toward the barn door.

"Why can't we just eat the medicine?" asked Little Kicker. "I want to eat mine." Little Kicker did not like the idea of anything poking through his donkey hide.

Little Kicker followed very slowly.

"Dear Lord," prayed Little Kicker quietly, "Please do not let the shot hurt very much. Thank you. Amen!"

Into the barn hopped Becky the Bunny with her two large ears stuffed into her little fireman's hat. Becky was happy. She planned to wiggle her ears. This would make her hat fly off so Little Kicker would laugh.

Farmer John bragged on Little Kicker. "This is our new donkey colt," he said proudly.

Doctor Quickwell opened his black leather doctor's bag. Sure enough, he pulled out a tube with a needle on the end just as Tony the Pony said.

Becky the Bunny's ears were too big for her fireman's hat. When she wiggled them, "Boing!" went the bunny ears as they sprang up. "Flip, flop and plop," went her fireman's hat. It sprang off Becky's head and landed on the barn floor.

The birdies sang, "Tweet, tweet, ha, ha!"

Little Kicker laughed big "Hee Haaws." He did not even feel the needle when Doctor Quickwell gave him the shot.

Doctor Quickwell left Little Kicker and walked to Tony the Pony.

"Hee, Haw! When is Doctor Quickwell going to give me my shot?" asked Little Kicker.

"He did give you the shot," said Mother Donkey. "He gave you the shot when you were laughing at Becky the Bunny."

Becky the Bunny picked up her hat. She was thrilled. Her plan had worked. She had made Little Kicker laugh.

Little Kicker giggled
"Hee Haw" giggles
as he walked out
of the barn with
Mother Donkey and
Tony the Pony.

"Mom," said Little Kicker, "I asked God to help me so the shot would not hurt very much."

"What happened?" asked Mother Donkey.

"The Lord answered my prayer," said Little Kicker. "He sent Becky the Bunny to make me laugh. God is my best helper."

"That's right, Little Kicker,"
replied Mother Donkey.

"God loves you very much. You
are special to the Lord, and you
are special to all of us."

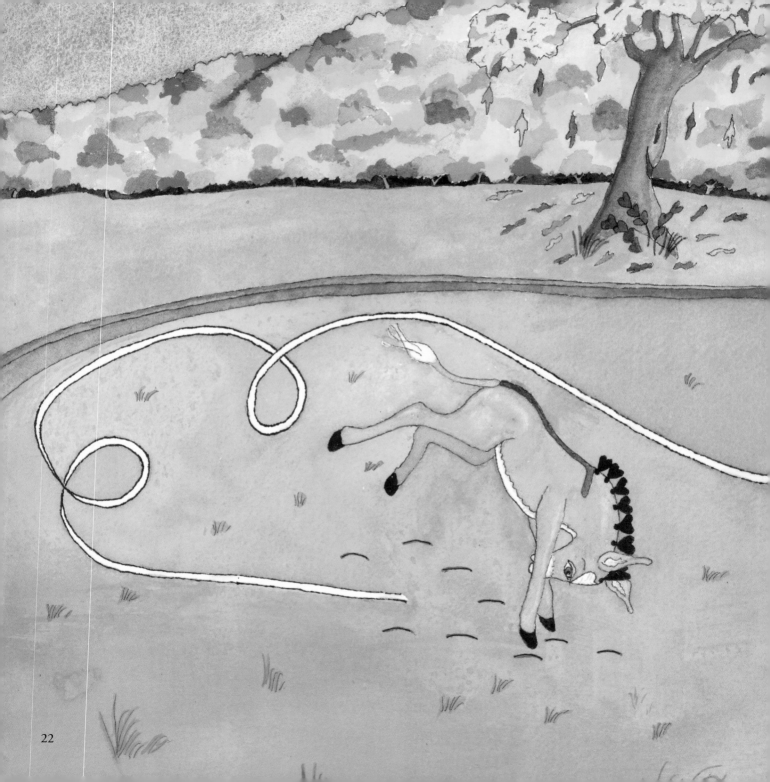

Little Kicker was sooo happy. He just
had to celebrate. Little Kicker ran
around in circles. He kicked and kicked
his back legs as high as they would go.

"Tony the Pony and Little Kicker ran to the new clover patch. Tony the Pony was happy. He stood up on his back legs and whinnied with joy.

"Hee Haw, Hee Haw," said Little Kicker as he nibbled on the clover. "It is wonderful to have God help us."

"Whinny," replied Tony the Pony, "it surely is. God loves us in a special way. In fact, God loves all children everywhere."

24

"I am glad God taught me to laugh at something funny when I get my shots," said Little Kicker. "I will always remember to do three things:"

1. "Pray that my shots will not hurt very much."

2. "Laugh, and"

3. "Not look at the needle."

25

funny Things I can Think about when I get a shot.

I LAUGH WHEN . . .

1) _____

2) _____

3) _____

LAUGHiNG ShOT AWARD

I LAUGHED DURING MY DOCTOR'S VISIT!

_____

NAME

_____

DATE

_____

DOCTOR OR NURSE

about Little Kicker Country

PLANTS AND ANIMALS OF THE OZARK MOUNTAIN REGION

Fun facts and insights for adults to learn and teach to
children about God's creation and provision

Viceroy Butterfly looks almost like the monarch. Monarchs
eat milkweed, which is bitter tasting. This discourages other
animals from eating them. This bitter flavor protects the
monarch and the look-alike viceroy from predators.

page 8

Killdeers are amusing ground nesting birds. When a threat
approaches their nest, killdeers will lower a wing so it looks
broken, squawk to attract attention and hobble away from their
nest. This leads predators away from their baby chicks.

Page 11 & 14

Barn Swallows are delightful birds and eat harmful insects as they fly
through the air. They reminded me of dive-bombers when they flew
through our barn doggie door then up to their nests. We love to watch
them in the evenings.

page 17

Red Clover is a wild plant and part of the legume family. Animals love eating it, and God designed it for many purposes. It has great food value and is used in many medications. It contains isoflavones and is believed to aid in fighting cancer, whooping cough, respiratory problems and skin conditions.

page 24

Tadpoles grow from frog eggs that were deposited in a slow part of the stream and attached to vegetation. The eggs hatch into tadpoles that swim away to feed. The tadpoles' long tails are absorbed into their bodies as they develop. When the maturing process is complete, they can hop onto land as a frog.

page 25

Milkweed Pods, when they are small and green, are used in many recipes. In the spring and summer the plant has green leaves and is a host for the monarch butterfly. In the late fall the pods turn brown, open and disperse their seeds.

page 12

history of the friends of Little Kicker

Sam the Lamb is named after my husband Sam. Being retired and fond of snoozing, he has a special snoozing spot on the map of Little Kicker Country. We celebrated our fiftieth in 2014.

Becky the Bunny is named after our daughter Becky. She has a hat for every occasion. Becky loves books and singing and helping others.

Tony the Pony is named after our son Tony. He is Little Kicker's best friend and the fastest thing on four hoofs. Tony has a great sense of humor.

Rachael the Little Red Hen is named for our granddaughter Rachael who had red hair when she was born. I painted the little hen with lots of hearts, which stand for all the love Rachael gives her family.

Tammy the Turtle is named after our daughter-in-law Tammy. We gladly added her to the list of animals when she joined our family. Tammy is sweet and always keeps her nails manicured.

Emma Cow is named after my dear mother Emma. She is the wise old sage in our books, and she taught me to love my Lord, Jesus Christ. Our daughter Becky named her calf Emma Cow.

Farmer John is a likeness of my Father who was a John Wayne type of man's man. My can-do attitude comes from him as well as from my mother.

Sandy the Sow Pig is named after me, your humble author. We both have green eyes, and we love being in the water. She likes to wallow in her mud holes, and I like to swim in the lake.

Fun Activities for Children

1. Ten up arrows are on the tree on page 6. Can you find them?

2. How many heart-shaped leaves are falling from the tree on page 8? How many leaves have already fallen on the ground?

3. Two shapes are on page 9. Can you point to the rectangle and the five ovals? Find the circle on page 17.

4. Many colors are on pages 10 and 11. How many of them can you name?

5. A triangle and a square (white salt block) are on page 19. Can you find them?

6. What is Little Kicker doing on pages 22 and 23?

7. How many frog eggs are in the water on page 25?

exciting, award-winning
LiTTLe KiCKer BOOKS®
♥ OUR READ-ALOUD SERIES ♥

A Prayer For Little Kicker
(Learning God has a special plan for my life)

Little Kicker's First Rainstorm
(Facing childhood fears)

Little Kicker Visits Doctor Quickwell (Preparing children for their doctor's visit and vaccinations)

Little Kicker Wants A Turn (A book about sharing and being sensitive to the needs of others)

Little Kicker Likes To Jump
(Being happy with the way God made me)

LiTTLe KiCKer's Life continues
♥ ILLUSTRATED CHAPTER BOOKS ♥

Little Kicker Learns it is Never Wrong to do the Right Thing

Little Kicker's Friendship Book
(Being happy with the friends God gave me)

Final chapter BOOK

Little Kicker Believes…
(God has a plan for him and for you.)

www.LiTTLeKiCKer.com
www.facebook.com/LiTTLeKiCKerBOOKS

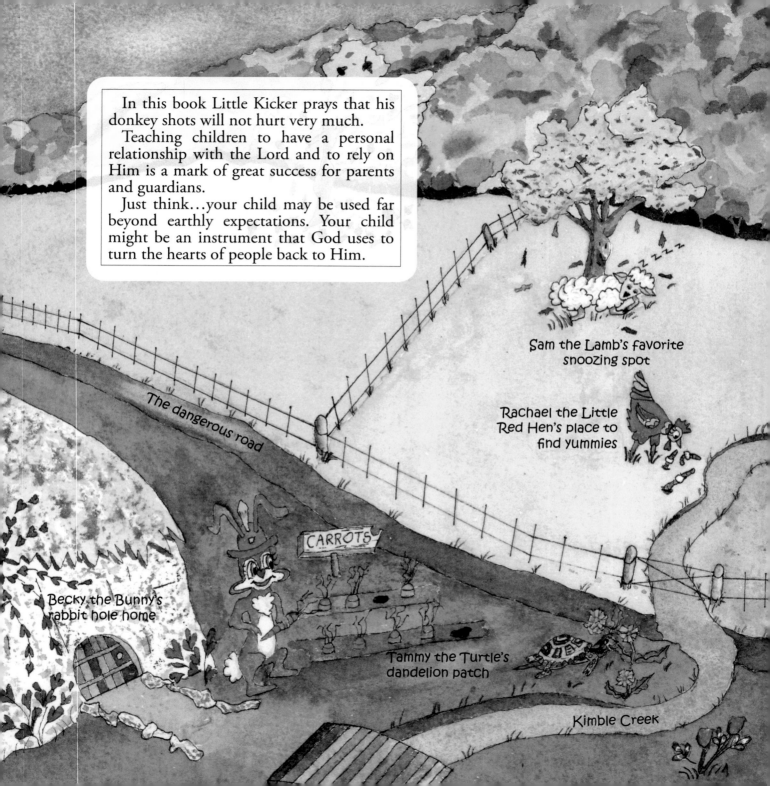

In this book Little Kicker prays that his donkey shots will not hurt very much.

Teaching children to have a personal relationship with the Lord and to rely on Him is a mark of great success for parents and guardians.

Just think…your child may be used far beyond earthly expectations. Your child might be an instrument that God uses to turn the hearts of people back to Him.

Sam the Lamb's favorite snoozing spot

Rachael the Little Red Hen's place to find yummies

The dangerous road

CARROTS

Becky the Bunny's rabbit hole home

Tammy the Turtle's dandelion patch

Kimble Creek